Praise for
The Adventures of Emery Jones,
Boy Science Wonder: Bending Time

A time-traveling lark written with energy and illustrated with terrific, deceptive simplicity, this hysterically funny story of young genius has serious things to say about friendship, bullying, identity, and the power of imagination. The kind of book parents will want to read to and with their children. If this is the beginning of a series, we are in for a genuine treat!

—Steve Barnes, science fiction author

Charles Johnson and Elisheba Johnson have done something special with *The Adventures of Emery Jones, Boy Science Wonder*. My prediction is that in twenty years' time it will not be uncommon to hear a scientist say that, as a kid, s/he was a fan of Emery Jones. I wish I could take this book back in time and give it to my younger self where it could spark my young imagination. I, for one, can't wait to see the impact these fictional characters, Emery Jones and his companion Gabby, have on the real world. Somewhere in the future there is a space probe or starship named the *Emery Jones*. I don't need a time machine to see that.

IcDonald, author of *Invisible Ink*

D0967326

The Adventures of Emery Jones, Boy Science Wonder contains everything its title implies. It's a great adventure tale, complete with monsters, journeys, and narrow escapes; it's a story of a heroic boy who is gifted at science; and, like all great children's writing, it is a tale of wonder. Charles and Elisheba Johnson have crafted a story where imagination matches science to create the splendor of possible worlds. Readers of all ages will lose themselves in this delightful, funny, insightful, and provocative story.

> —Marc Conner, Associate Provost, Ballengee Professor of English, Washington & Lee University, author of *Charles Johnson: The Novelist as Philosopher* and founding member of the Charles Johnson Society

Emery Jones has multiple levels of concepts and ideas that need to be discussed. I like that one character has a disability—and it has to do with hearing. This book might just teach a generation of young people to learn sign language. You've given us a children's book that leans against the pillars of research. Much an adult can learn from reading this book too.

> —Ethelbert Miller, poet

Bending Time is a rollicking good read, with vividly drawn characters, a pleasingly rapid pace, an engaging narrative voice, and wonderful illustrations. It's sure to leave readers with plenty to think about, and not just in the realm of science. It's furthermore an auspicious debut for *The Adventures of Emery Jones, Boy Science Wonder* series. Authors Charles and Elisheba Johnson offer, in *Bending Time*, delight and edification on every page. I look forward to subsequent volumes.

> —David Guterson, author of *Snow Falling on Cedars*

BENDING TIME

THE ADVENTURES OF EMERY JONES, BOY SCIENCE WONDER

Written by Charles Johnson & Elisheba Johnson
Illustrated by Charles Johnson

A WORK FROM THE
JOHNSON CONSTRUCTION CO.

booktrope

Booktrope Editions
Seattle, WA 2013

Written by Charles Johnson & Elisheba Johnson
Illustrated by Charles Johnson
Cover Design by Rob Johnson

This is a work of fiction. Names, characters, places, brands, media, and incidents are either the product of the authors' imagination or are used fictitiously. Any resemblance to similarly named places or to persons living or deceased is unintentional.

PRINT ISBN 978-1-62015-181-5
EPUB ISBN 978-1-62015-277-5

For further information regarding permissions, please contact info@booktrope.com.

Library of Congress Control Number: 2013917025

ACKNOWLEDGMENTS

Acknowledgment is gratefully made to the books and people without whom this story could not have been written. Of special importance for its theory of time travel is Dr. Ronald L. Mallett's *Time Traveler*. My daughter and I must also acknowledge my indebtedness to filmmaker Art Washington for his helpful suggestions throughout the process of this book's creation, and for dutifully reading and commenting on many drafts as I passed them by him.

These words were collaged for your ears.

For Elisheba's son and Charles's grandson,

Emery Charles Spearman.

The first time I saw Emery Jones was last year when we were in fourth grade. Most kids meet their best friends on the playground or quietly in class. Not me. What I remember is a big-headed boy about four foot ten in a dark blue blazer, wearing black sneakers, a striped tie, and tan trousers with cuffs, barreling down the hallway, shoving all the kids in the hallway aside.

"Move!" he shouted. "They're after me!" He had a camera and a notepad. Right behind him was the Lunch Lady, waving a frying pan, screaming, "Get him before he gets us all fired!"

He stopped right in front of me in the crowded hallway, breathing hard. The tail of his shirt was hanging outside his trousers. One of his shoelaces was untied. "Help me!" he said. "I need somewhere to hide!"

I had just opened my locker. "You can go in there...I guess."

He squeezed inside, then pulled the door shut. I stood with my back pressed against the locker just as the Lunch Lady came barreling around the corner.

"Where is he?" she said. "I know he came this way!"

I turned up my hearing aid. "Who?"

"That skinny boy with the big glasses and all them crazy gadgets."

I shrugged my shoulders. "I don't know, ma'am." I gave her my sweetest little girl look. Grown-ups always fell for that. The Lunch Lady huffed and puffed, said whoever this Emery was would be the ruin of Moms Mabley Elementary School, then she went galumphing off down the hallway, swearing she would first call her lawyer, then the school board, and finally the mayor if he didn't stop whatever it was he was doing.

Once she was gone, Emery stepped out of my locker, looking up and down the hallway to make sure he was in the clear. I asked him, "What was all *that* about?"

"Yesterday, I saw something funny-looking in that mystery meat they served us for lunch." He flipped open his notebook to show me what he had written. "I decided to do my own investigation. I started testing things this morning and taking pictures. Right when I was testing the meat, in comes Lunch Lady Montgomery. She grabbed a pot, started waving it at me, and said, 'Children can't be in the kitchen!' I'm going to expose them. Look, I grabbed some meat to run tests on."

I looked down at a green-hued piece of hamburger patty in his palm. My stomach flipped. This kid was on to something.

"We could all get sick if we eat this slop! I think you should bring your own food and bottled water from now on."

"What are you going to do?"

"Send all the evidence I gather to Principal Jackson. Maybe he can make conditions in the cafeteria better." As he talked, his glasses kept sliding down his nose. He pushed them up with two fingers, and then shook my hand. "Thanks for letting me use your locker. I'm Emery."

"Any time," I said. "I'm Gabby."

That was a year ago. And actually my name is Gwen, but everybody calls me Gabby, because that's what I'm not. I don't talk much unless I've got something really important to say. And what I want to say right now isn't about me at all. Well, not exactly. It's more about what happened to us—and you—this school year because of some bullies.

But I'll get to that in a minute.

The important thing you need to know is that it wasn't easy being Emery Jones. People told him he had too much imagination.

Can you believe that? Everyone from his parents to people at school said he ought to be medicated. What if they'd done that to Beethoven or Isaac Newton? The Lunch Lady said imagining things and being nosy would get him in trouble. I guess she was right. After Principal Jackson confronted her about bad food on the school's menu, she barred Emery from the cafeteria for the rest of the year.

If that wasn't bad enough, the other kids thought he was a little weird. He was always reading and got as bony as a starved cat because he'd forget to eat when his head was buried in the *Journal of Mathematical Physics*. I enjoyed the fact that he was forever tinkering with things, taking them apart to see how they worked and putting them back together again differently—like the time he remade my plastic hearing aid so strong that I could pick up on what people were saying way across a room. (Of course, I don't turn it up that high most of the time because I don't like listening in on folks without their permission.) Without it, I can't hear anything. It's like my ears are stuffed with cotton. My parents made me learn sign language. Emery learned it, too, so he could talk to me.

The problem was that he never seemed able to leave well enough alone. Being his good friend, I let him know whenever I thought he was getting too far out there or showing off by telling you the day of the week going back to 2001 if you gave him a date. I told him when he needed a reality check.

Isn't that what friends are for?

Maybe that's what I should have done a couple of months ago when Mr. Tiplightly, our science teacher, asked the question that got us into so much trouble and turned our world upside down. He'd already taught us about how the dinosaurs were probably killed off by meteor showers that lasted two million years.

"Can anyone tell me what came after the dinosaurs?" he asked.

The room was quiet. It was a nine o'clock class. Everybody looked sleepy or was dozing off. At the back of the room, Chippy Payne, who stood head and shoulders above the rest of us ten-year-olds, had his head down on his desk; his buddy

Pookie Wilson, who let his pants hang down below his butt so you could see his underwear, was snoring; and his other friend, Toughie McDonald, who never used deodorant, was sticking his right hand into his armpit, pulling it out, then smelling his fingers to see if he had any bad odors (he did) and needed a bath.

Every time old Mr. Tiplightly looked at them, he gave a big sigh. He shook his head in disapproval when Pookie made hand farts. I figure Mr. Tiplightly had been around as long as dirt. The back of his neck puckered out in two bulges. To me, he seemed like one of the big, soft toads he had us dissect in class. Or an old baby. As far as I could tell, he hadn't opened a science book any younger than we were. But he liked talking about science because it was full of facts you couldn't argue with. Let me say that again more clearly: He didn't like you arguing with *him*, because he always needed to be right.

But scientists dream like poets. Like philosophers. Like Emery. They were adventurous. They tossed around exciting theories. Our teacher always tipped lightly around those.

"Anybody know the answer?" Mr. Tiplightly asked again.

Emery was sitting with his left elbow on his desk, his chin resting on his palm. He raised his right hand.

"There were several times the dinosaurs died off. Two times were right before and after the Triassic period. Back then," he said, "all the lands on Earth were mashed together in one big supercontinent called Pangaea."

Mr. Tiplightly smiled. "Well, I guess somebody's been reading our textbook."

"No, I saw one yesterday."

"You saw a dinosaur in a book?"

"No, sir."

"On television or at a museum then?"

"No, I saw it in the..." Emery hesitated, realizing he'd said too much. "I've seen a real one. Trust me."

Mr. Tiplightly gave him one of those severe teacher looks, the kind that can fry you in your seat. "Emery, you have a right to your own beliefs, not to your own facts. There are no dinosaurs today. And no one can see or travel backward in time."

21

"But some things, like positrons, do travel backward in time. You know about them, right?"

Mr. Tiplightly coughed into his right hand. "Of course, I know what they are."

It was pretty obvious that he didn't.

"No one knows what time is." Emery talked with his hands whenever he explained something, like sign language and speech at the same time. That day his fingers were flying. "Einstein wrote in a 1955 letter that 'People like us, who believe in physics, know that the distinction between past, present, and future is only a stubbornly persistent illusion.'" He was getting that dreamy look in his eyes again. "Nothing is impossible. Nothing we think we know is certain. And everything that can happen *does* happen. You need to think outside the box, sir."

"Oh, I'd say one thing is certain," said Mr. Tiplightly.

"What?"

"The effect that gravity is having on your grade this morning."

That made the whole class crack up. They acted like Emery had come to school with his sweater on backwards. He slumped down in his seat, chin drooped on his chest. He didn't say a word for the rest of the class, but with his fingers he signed to me, *I did see one.*

The bell rang. Emery still had his head down when he hurried out the door, a booger and a lump of pink bubble gum that Chippy put on his chair stuck to the seat of his pants. They were still there when school was over. Chippy and his crew—they hung together like flies—were right behind us as we walked home.

"Gizmo, you need to quit thinkin' outside the box." He threw a right cross at Emery, who ducked—we all ducked a lot when Chippy was around—while Pookie snatched his book bag, dumping it out on the ground covered with October leaves. Toughie filmed them on his cell phone so that later he could put it on the Internet and have everyone laugh at Emery. "What you need to worry about is how you're ever gonna survive fifth grade."

Emery mumbled under his breath, "I'll bet you can't even spell fifth grade."

"What's that, Gizmo?"

"I'm so sick of this!" I shouted. "Leave us alone!" I started searching the ground for a dookey-stick to hit him with, though I knew it wouldn't do much good. He was thick as a brick. "He's not bothering you."

Even though those three were bullies, they thought twice about ruining their reputation by hitting a girl with a hearing aid. They made me so mad sometimes. They tripped Emery. They poked him. They pushed him down stairs. They teased him if he used a word they didn't know. They were always wolfing at him because he wasn't good at defending himself with an equally insulting reply. (Like his mother, he didn't even cuss; he walked out of movies after the second swear word.)

Pookie, looking at Emery's shoes, would say, "You got them shoes from Buster Brown, didn't you? Brown on top and busted on the bottom."

Then Toughie started on him. "Yo' house so small, Emery, the roaches got to walk single file."

By then they'd be laughing so hard that strings of snot hung out of their noses. Chippy was always the one to cap on him last.

"How tall are you, Gizmo?"

"Five feet. Or one-point-five meters."

"I didn't know garbage piled that high."

Maybe I shouldn't be too hard on Pookie. He had a shiny bald head as smooth as an eggshell except for his Mohawk, talked out of the side of his mouth, and had this big

bacon-grease burn on his arm. Was that why he acted so mean? And maybe I should lighten up on Toughie, too. He didn't act bad all the time; in fact, he was so cute it was hard to believe sometimes that he was a boy. I guess he acted tough so you wouldn't notice his black, curly eyelashes, long springy hair, and his dimples the size of dimes.

Whatever. Enough about them.

Because it was that loser Chippy who upset me most: the way he talked loud with a strut in his voice, took up so much space when he came in the room, his New York Giants cap cocked to one side on his head, looking shifty-eyed over his shoulder like he'd stolen something (which he probably had), and then everything he said, things he didn't say — everything!

I watched them walk away, like they thought they owned the sidewalk. I helped Emery put his homework papers back into his bag. He didn't look me in the eye when he said, "Thanks for sticking up for me. You're the only person I can talk to. You and Professor Haley."

I nodded my head. "It's because we're different."

That was something I knew about him ever since the teachers gave us an IQ test and Emery scored 188. He could learn any language in fourteen days. Like President James Garfield, he was able to write Latin with one hand and Greek with the other at the same time. He was super good at that science, technology, engineering, and math stuff. One week when he was bored, he taught himself calculus, algebra, geometry, and trigonometry. When he dreamed, it was in computer code. But why is it that no one ever tells you that being different means people will see you as being strange. Or wrong. Maybe even dangerous. He tried to play with other kids our age, and he got bored pretty fast. So we didn't have many friends, me because of my disability and him because there were so few people who understood him. Other kids didn't invite us to their parties. We were lonely lots of times. So he would always listen for as long as I wanted to talk. That's more than I can say for his parents.

Don't get me wrong. His dad is an okay, easygoing guy who grew up in the country. He has the kind of toothbrush moustache Charlie Chaplin wore in the movies. He likes to bet on the horses and play the lottery. When he was younger, no one taught him table manners, so he drinks hot coffee with a tablespoon, slurping up the black stuff like he was eating soup, his belly sticking outside the buttons of his shirt. The way he ate made me and Emery laugh because Mr. Jones hung his head over his plate, packing so much food into his mouth all at once that his cheeks ballooned out like a chipmunk's.

Seeing him do that made Emery's mom, who is real proper, look like she wanted to scream. I could tell it embarrassed Emery, too. His mom tried to set a good example by never letting food fall from her fork, which she lifted to her lips in a way as delicate as Mrs. Bernice Jones was herself, thin and fragile like a porcelain doll or a china teacup. She wiped her mouth carefully with a napkin after every two or three bites. On the other hand, his father—a proud, stubborn Southern man—wasn't about to change his ways.

Sometimes his dad, who dropped out of high school when he was sixteen and hadn't cracked open a book since then, wasn't okay at all.

He liked the improvements Emery was always making around their house. But whenever he showed his Dad one of his latest inventions, Mr. Jones would turn his eyes away from being glued to his favorite wrestling smackdown show and just grunt,

"I guess that's all right." He never told him what he was doing was good. Or even that he was proud of him. Whenever Emery started a conversation about a subject his father didn't understand (which was a lot of the time), Mr. Jones would cut him off and suddenly remember something he needed to do in another room. One time when we were eating Sunday dinner, I heard him tell Emery that too much brain work wasn't good for you and might make you go crazy.

That made his mom slap her hand down on the table. Her fingertips hit the edge of her plate, tilting it so food flew straight into the air. Green peas rained down on us. I thought she was going to explode.

"Curtis, mind how you talk to this boy!"

His dad turtled his head into the collar of the green work shirt he wore as a night watchman at the city yards. "Honey, I was just sayin'..."

"Something wrong! I want our son to be everything he can be. Maybe even more than we can dream of."

I liked Emery's mom, though she couldn't help him much. Whenever he tried to talk to her about his homework or some new discovery he was excited about, his mom, who was a nurse's aide, got confused. He had more book learning than both his parents put together. She was a little frightened by him, worried about his future. She didn't know how best to help him, at least not the way Professor Haley did.

Dangerfield Edison Haley just might be the greatest scientist you never heard about. They met at one of those science fairs where Emery was always winning prizes, and the Professor took him under his wing because he was kinda like Emery, always looking at strange things like somehow he felt he knew them, and at things he knew perfectly well as if he wasn't sure about them at all. Although he won a Nobel Prize in something way before we were born, he was so private he didn't even go to the award ceremony in Norway. Ordinary things made him yawn. He liked to quote philosopher William James saying, "The essence of genius is knowing what to overlook." (Mr. Jones hated it when the Professor quoted from books; when Emery did that, he grumped, "Why don't you repeat the things *I* say?") Overlooking things is probably what got Professor Haley fired from the university, because he forgot some days to teach his classes when he was wrapped up in his experiments. He overlooked a lot. Emery told me that once when he bought something and got a fifty-dollar bill back as change, he just used it as a bookmark, then forgot it was there when he took the book back to the library. At times he made me think of those fairy tale wizards with mischievous, twinkling eyes or a leprechaun living on the earnings from patents for all the things he'd invented, and other times he reminded me of a gray-haired, playful old grandpa.

But I still didn't understand what Emery said in class about seeing prehistoric creatures. So instead of asking about that, I slowed down a step to adjust my underwear because it felt bunched up. I said, "You, I understand. What I wish I understood better are my history lessons. All I'm good at is writing stories in my English class."

Emery smiled. "I'm going to prove what I told Mr. Tiplightly. Then you can use what I made for your history homework."

Before I could say anything, he was off running to his house. It was in a poor neighborhood near a junk yard, but where you live is what you make of it. He spent lots of time in that junk yard and at dumps and garage sales, thinking, *What if those old computers and electronic equipment people tossed aside could be used for something else?* And anything he couldn't find, Professor

Haley got for him. All those thrown-away items let him trick out his parents' place as one of those smart houses where electronics controlled everything. There were solar panels on the roof, little six-legged, spiderlike robots that ran the dishwasher, lights, folded the laundry, and cleaned the floors. (So it didn't have any cockroaches like Toughie said. There wasn't even a speck of dust or a bread crumb on the floor.) But his favorite invention of all was Caliban, the rapping robot he programmed to speak all the 6,900 languages in the world and spit the best rhymes.

His mom worked long hours. She got home just as his dad was leaving for work, so they were never there when he came in from school, but the house let him right in when he pressed his hand on a pad by the front door that recognized his fingerprints. Later he told me that upstairs in his bedroom, he went to work finishing the thing he promised to bring to school.

Then the next day I saw it. Right before science class when we were standing outside, waiting for Mr. Tiplightly to open the door. Emery had wheeled it to school on a little red Radio Flyer wagon. I just stared at it. It took my breath away. Whatever it was, it was beautiful.

No, that word *beautiful* isn't right. A better word is the one Emery used when he talked about those head-breaking equations he loved: *elegant*. His invention was a clear glass cylinder, half as big as him, with another cylinder inside and lots of mirrors. On the top was a screen, a keyboard marked with Greek and science symbols, switches, levers, and dials. It looked more like a work of modern art than a machine. For a second it made me think about how everything that people made—the school, my shoes, the red wagon it rested on—started out first as an idea in somebody's imagination. Ideas weren't physical at all. Wasn't that magic, then? Nothing becoming something?

"What does it do?" I asked.

"I'm not sure yet about everything it does." Emery took a second to swallow. "You know how television works, right? Electrons let you create, then send signals across space. I was thinking about that, fooling around with a laser I built, mirrors and rotating cylinders that bent light back on itself, and I caused a closed time-curve, and out of nowhere I started receiving signals from the past."

"Em," I sighed. "That's way too much information. I ask you what time it is, and you tell me how to build a clock. Talk English, please."

"It lets me see things that used to be. It's like the Chronovisor Father Marcello Pellegrino Ernetti, a Benedictine monk, said he built in the 1950s, which let him see into the past or future. Father Ernetti supposedly created it with a group of scientists that included physicist Enrico Fermi and rocket scientist Wernher von Braun, but it was kept hidden by the Vatican. No one knows if any of this is true. But my invention is real. It was only a little harder than building a ham radio."

"Well, for you maybe...."

"After I show it to Mr. Tiplightly, I'll let you borrow it, so when you have a history lesson you can study people in that time and place."

I was about to thank him when Chippy stepped up behind us. He snatched the invention out of Emery's hands.

"What you got there, Gizmo?" He held it up high so Emery couldn't reach it. "You still playin' with toys?"

Then he did what he shouldn't have done. He started pushing keys and throwing switches.

"No!" Emery shouted.

That made Chippy turn dials and pull levers even harder. The inner and outer

cylinders began to rotate in opposite directions, faster and faster. The little screen kept flashing. I could see snatches of times past—the Civil War, Egyptians building the pyramids, then things that looked like cavemen.

Even though Chippy was laughing nervously, I saw the smile on his face going south. "Is this some kind of TV or DVD player?"

Then something happened that was unreal. A hole opened in time. The screen froze on a place I'd never seen before, and the rotating lights inside the cylinder created a big flash of light like an explosion in a fireworks factory, so bright it filled the hallway, blinding me.

When I could see again, Chippy was gone.

Emery's invention was broken, melted down to smoking pieces of glass in the wagon. Behind me, I heard a voice say, "What was *that*?"

It was Mr. Tiplightly. "What did you two do to him? You blew him up, didn't you?"

"No!" said Emery.

"Then where is he? How did this happen? Whose problem is this?"

"I—" Emery's voice broke off.

Before we could say another word, Mr. Tiplightly grabbed us each by the collar and hauled us to Principal Jackson's office. He said Emery had brought a dangerous device to school, that he'd done away with Chippy.

We said, no, that wasn't true. Or was it? I didn't like Chippy one bit, but the last thing I wanted was for him to be dead.

Now, if there was anything Principal Jackson hated, it was someone handing him a problem. "That's the only time anyone ever comes to visit me," he once said. "When something goes wrong." If someone brought him a problem, he had a way of slowing down, getting quieter, so he could cope with it. He talked slow. He moved in slow motion, breathing like air leaking out of a bicycle tire with a nail stuck in it. Speaking of nails, at the start of the school year when he welcomed us in the auditorium, Principal Jackson said problems were just like nails sticking out of the floor. "And the nail that sticks up," he said, "must be hammered down."

He brought that hammer down hard on both of us.

"We're *expelled*?" Emery was as shocked as I was.

"Yes, if we can't find Clarence Earl Payne Jr. Do you know where he is?"

"Not exactly," Emery said, thinking fast. "But I saw him leave the building through one of the exits to escape all the smoke. He has to be outside now. Maybe he went home...."

Principal Jackson rubbed his nose in slo-mo, seeing Emery's explanation as possible. He still had a problem, though, and he wasn't pleased. "Mr. Jones, this is the third time this year that you've been brought to my office. Your stock is sinking very fast at Moms Mabley Elementary School. I'm going to call your parents. We're going to notify the police and start searching for Mr. Payne right now. Consider yourself expelled from this school. If we don't find him, you and Gwendolyn Sykes may be charged with kidnapping or murder."

I felt like I was going to faint. I shut off my hearing aid so I wouldn't have to listen anymore. I shoved my fist in my mouth to keep from screaming. Wasn't enough wrong with my life already? Didn't I have enough things not to like about myself? Some of the girls at school were developing hourglass figures, but I was still a clunky, almond-eyed apple with two pigtails that fell just past my shoulders.

I looked at Emery. Emery looked at me. We both looked at the open door, then we flew through it, running so fast neither old Mr. Tiplightly or slow-moving Principal Jackson could keep up with us.

We didn't stop running until we got to a park halfway to Emery's house.

I signed, *What're we going to do?*

He was leaning against a tree, breathing hard. With two fingers, he pushed his glasses higher on his nose. "I can fix this. I can put this toothpaste back in the tube. We just need to get to my house."

"What happened to Chippy?"

"I thought what I made just received visual signals from the past. But it's a transceiver, receiving and transmitting objects, too. There's still something I can't figure out, though...."

"Em, you're doing it again! I ask you a ten-second question and you start giving me a twenty-minute answer. Speak English!"

"I sent him back in time. I didn't know it could do that." His fingers kneaded his lower lip. "I think I can reverse the process, but we have to hurry...."

We ran so hard, one of my shoes flew off my foot. As much as I liked those shoes I got for my birthday, I didn't go back for it, and ran. Ran past the mini-marts two blocks from where he lived, past abandoned cars and garbage piled on the streets. I was just glad when that smart house of his let us in.

"Karibu." Cal the robot welcomed us inside with conversational Swahili.

"Switch to American," said Emery.

"I need to brush up on my Swahili grammar."

"We can do that some other time."

Once inside, I relaxed a little. I loved seeing the bedroom where Emery worked. It was so junky. You could see everything that was inside his head. Or close to his heart. On his desk he had a little model of one of Leonardo da Vinci's flying machines. Next to that was a small model of the *Opportunity* Mars rover right beside a rotating model of all the planets in our solar system. He used a thumb-sized piece of a meteorite as a paperweight.

Over his desk, on all four walls, there were posters of his heroes smiling down at you: astrophysicist Neil deGrasse Tyson, physicist Ronald L. Mallett, astronaut Ron McNair, and that peanut guy, George Washington Carver. There was also one of Mahatma Gandhi saying, "First they ignore you. Then they laugh at you. Then they fight you. Then you win."

Emery went right to work, pulling all kinds of stuff out of his closet as he looked for something: screwdrivers, video cards, calculators, beakers, glass cutters, blueprints, tongs, motherboards, a micrometer, an electron microscope, hard drives. At last he found, way in the back, what he was looking for.

It was a glass cylinder like the one he brought to school. The only difference was

that it looked less finished. Less polished.
Emery called it a prototype—a version of the
time transceiver he built before the one I
saw. He put on safety glasses and gloves,
then began tightening screws on it as Cal
rolled into the bedroom, blinking, clanking,
and holding a tray.

Emery Jones, you're skin and bones.
Missed breakfast, lunch, and dinner.
That's no way to be a winner.
All that does is make you thinner.

"Not now, Cal." He didn't look up from
what he was doing. "I'm busy."

Listen, I've got vitamins A, C, D, and E!
These are for you, not for me!
I know when you're working, you don't
    give a hoot.
But these bad boys will help your brain
    reboot.

"Okay, okay!" Emery yanked off one glove. Scooping his vitamins off the tray, he flicked them into his mouth like popcorn.

Ms. Gwen, it's good to see you again.
You look a little tired, or maybe it's wired.
I can bring a glass of milk to help you chill.
Or if you like, put a burger on the grill.

"Thanks, Cal. I'm fine. You know, Em, you need to program Cal for better raps. I know he's a robot, but—"

"That's on my to-do list. For later."

I watched Emery work, handing him the tools he asked for when he said *pliers* or *wrench.* Once he'd made all the adjustments he wanted to the prototype, he crossed the fingers on his left hand. With his free hand, he began tapping keys, throwing switches and turning dials in the order Chippy had done. The inner and outer cylinders rotated, flooding his bedroom with light. The house rocked on its foundations, throwing pictures off the walls and books from their shelves. However, this transceiver didn't explode or melt into a puddle of smoking glass. It made a steady humming sound. On its screen was the last image I'd seen before Chippy disappeared from the hallway at school.

A prehistoric world of shocks. Of mysteries. I saw a dark, steaming swamp crawling with critters. Reptiles. A bat-winged lizard soared across a silver moon so huge it seemed only half the distance from the earth that it is today. Far away, a volcano spewed out soot, scorching the sky. There, closer by in the moonlight, I saw Chippy crouched beneath fallen trees covered with moss as green as mold on bread, 190 million years away from anything he was sure about. Even though where he was looked steamy-hot, he was shivering, hunched into himself, trying to hide as a prowling lizard as big as our school bus lumbered by.

Right then, a really bad thought hit me. "What if he changes something back there? Won't that change the future—I mean, the present where we are now?"

"Don't worry," said Emery. "You can't change the past. Something will always happen to keep things as they are."

I noticed uncertainty in his voice. "Are you sure? Nothing is going to be changed?"

"Gabby," yelped Chippy, "is that *you*? Where are you? Where am *I*?"

"He can see and hear us. How can he do that?"

Emery tapped the end of his nose, pacing his bedroom in a circle as he thought it through. "There must be a transceiver where he is. I guess I didn't create a time machine after all. I just completed half of one. The other half is providing the connection between the past and our present. It must have been running all this time, turned on during the Mesozoic era, waiting for someone like me to create a receiver."

"Turned on by who?"

"I dunno." He raised his shoulders in a shrug. "Chippy, listen to me carefully, okay? You're in Pangaea. That's in the Triassic period. There are no humans there, just you. Dinosaurs are still early in their development."

"Oh, *really*? Guess what, Gizmo. One has been chasing me, trying to eat me ever since I got here!"

"Stay calm. We're going to figure out a way to get you home. But I need you to do something."

"What? I'll do anything if it'll get me out of here."

"Find some dinosaur poop. Cover yourself with it from head to toe."

"No way!"

"It's the *only* way. You know how dogs behave. They don't hang around a bush where they peed or pooped. If you smell like them, they'll leave you alone."

Chippy screwed his face up in a frown. He replied by dropping his pants. His boxers. Then he mooned us.

I signed so Chippy couldn't hear us. *Is what you said for real? Will that keep dinosaurs from eating him?*

Who knows? I just want to see Chippy covered in dinosaur doo-doo.

"That's wrong!" I blurted out. "That's so wrong! He needs your help."

Emery got quiet for a moment. He took off his glasses, which meant he was looking my way without really seeing me. I was out of focus. As he spoke, he was talking less to me than out loud to himself. "I think we should leave him in the Triassic period. That'll serve him right. You know he's been beating up on me since we were in kindergarten. Because of him, there were days I didn't want to go to school. I lied. I told my parents

I felt sick on those days. He made me feel so bad I couldn't study. I cried myself to sleep. Once or twice I thought about killing myself. But I knew I had to be better than the bullies and haters said I was. If we leave him in the past, that's one less person in the present to make me feel like I'm a failure or a freak or always wrong."

I couldn't say anything because I knew what he was talking about. All our lives, people had made us feel bad because something about us was different. We were the crooked nails people always tried to hammer down.

"I feel the same way you do," I said. "But if you don't bring him back, we'll be expelled. Principal Jackson said we'd be charged with kidnapping. Or even murder! Maybe you don't care. You told me once you felt every day you spent at that school made your IQ drop by two points. But I want to finish, go on to Redd Foxx Middle School, to Richard Pryor High, then college! Not to prison...."

"Professor Haley says schools are just tools. He told me we have to go beyond our teachers. That's how we honor them."

"Well, fine! But can we at least graduate first?"

He kept staring down at the floor, like he was concentrating or studying the pattern of the carpet. He rubbed his face with both hands, then wiped his glasses on the end of his striped tie, slowly bobbing his head up and down.

"You're right. I'll go back for him." He let out a long sigh. "I need your help, though. And there's something I'd better get from the refrigerator."

Emery went downstairs to the kitchen. He came back a few minutes later with a big paper sack tucked under his right arm. From the clutter of his bedroom, he found a gadget attached to a lightbulb. He snapped it onto his belt, then moved his feet back and forth on the carpet so his body charged it with static electricity—30,000 volts, he said. He closed his eyes for a moment to pull his thoughts together.

"There are a lot of instruments on this control panel. Don't worry about what they do. I memorized the dials, levers, switches, and keys Chippy accidentally activated that displaced him in time. So I can go where he is. We can rescue him. Like I said, we can unring this bell if you activate these instruments in reverse order to get us back here. Can you do that?"

"I think so," I said, but I wasn't sure. I didn't have a photographic memory or see numbers in bright colors the way he did. People call that synesthesia. "I'll try."

"*Try* isn't good enough. If you get the sequence wrong, we'll be in the Triassic period forever. You'll be charged with two kidnappings. No going to the Richard Pryor High School prom."

"I'll do it."

His lips turned up in a triangle that made his eyes twinkle. He was trusting me with his life.

Isn't that what friends are for?

Emery showed me what I was supposed to do. I wrote it down on a notepad, which I placed beside the transceiver. "You better step out into the hallway. The time transport area covers half a meter." His fingers fluttered, *Wish me luck.*

I watched him quickly yank levers, crank dials, flip switches, and tap the keyboard, playing it like a piano. The cylinders rotated faster. Light brighter than the sun washed through his bedroom, melting away every shadow. I turned my head. I shielded my eyes with one hand. There came a sound like a thunderclap.

He was gone.

I'd been holding my breath. I let it out slowly, stepping back into the bedroom, wanting to see if Emery was in that prehistoric swamp. Then something stopped me. I heard as if from far away police sirens breaking the room's silence. I hurried to the bedroom window and pulled back the curtain. I saw police cars. Fire trucks. An ambulance. Emery's transceiver hadn't just sent him back in time. It was interfering with every cell tower within a half-mile radius of his house, disrupting signals, fouling up radio frequencies. Cell phones went kaput. Computers inside cars were failing to recognize codes sent by transponders in ignition keys. Neighbors spilled from their houses to stare. Over my head I heard the *whup, whup, whup* of a news helicopter. I felt a shiver prickle up the skin on my back. Were all those people looking for us?

"Cal," I said.

"Yes, Ms. Gwen?"

The little robot rolled toward the window.

"What are we going to do?"

I don't suggest we fool around.
I've already locked the doors and windows
    down.

"But," I said, "Emery's parents may be
out there..."

If I let them in, Emery will be perturbed,
Said when he's working, he's not to be
    disturbed.
Just to be sure no one enters this space,
I'm activating the electric barrier around
    the place.
And Ms. Gwen, if you're really his friend,
You'll stop all this blether and pull
    yourself together.

"Oh, button your lip! Cal, sometimes
you're too bossy! It's not cute!"

He muted his chatter. I went back to the transceiver. There, I saw a doo-doo-covered Chippy screaming, sprinting for all he was worth from that giant lizard. He ran, his knees pumping, and twisted his foot. He cried out in pain. Suddenly, Emery burst out of the bushes between them. He threw the bag he'd brought in the dinosaur's path, then helped Chippy get to his feet. The dinosaur stopped, poking its snout against the bag. When it saw what spilled out, it started to eat.

Chippy limped along, leaning on Emery. He looked back in wonder.

"You gave it a salad? It eats veggies?"

"It's a Plateosaurus," Emery said. "A herbivore. They only eat plants. You weren't in much danger."

68

"Thanks for telling me now." I thought Chippy was about to get mad, to take a swing at Emery again. Instead, he looked real hard at him, like he was seeing him for the first time. Heavily, he sat down on a huge fallen tree, rubbing his sore ankle.

"You came back for me?"

"Yeah."

"Why'd you do that?"

Emery sat down beside him. "I had to." He looked at Chippy's ankle. "Are you okay?"

"Okay? No, I'm *not* okay! What'd you think, Brickhead! Everythin' here is too big. Too strange. I feel like I'm gonna get squashed by somethin' any minute. I'm not sure how I got here, but I know I don't belong here."

"Now you know how I feel every day." He started to reach out to pat Chippy on his shoulder, but thought better of it. "We should examine the transceiver that brought us here so we can get back home."

"What if I don't want to go back."

"Huh?"

"I don't want to stay here. I'm askin' if there's any way you can send me to some other time."

"Why?"

"Where we came from...I don't belong there either. Remember when we were in second grade?"

"Yeah...you beat me up every other day."

"Well, I guess I shouldn't have done that. But that's nothin' compared to how my

71

momma beats me." The muscles around his mouth tightened. "We were walkin' down the street once, coming from the grocery store. We passed by an alley. I saw this drunk, homeless man in dirty, raggedy clothes. He had a runny nose, no shoes. He was diggin' through a garbage can. Dumpster divin'. He was eatin' and drinkin' whatever he could find that wasn't spoiled or stinkin' too bad. I don't know why, but I burst out laughin'. I couldn't help myself. I guess I laughed because I didn't want to start cryin'. That was when my Momma slapped me so hard I saw stars. 'Don't you make fun of him,' she said. 'He's your father.'"

That stopped Emery cold. "Your father?"

Chippy gave a head-shake. "When I found out who he was, I wanted to talk to him. But my momma wouldn't let me. So that's the only time I ever saw him. That one time made me feel ashamed. It made me feel all broken up inside. And that made me want to break things. What I figured out is that when people were afraid of me, they left me alone. They didn't make me feel bad about my father or anythin' else. My momma is always sayin' I'm gonna wind up just like him. Or in jail. 'Like father, like son,' she's always sayin'. I don't want that. So no way do I want to go back to where we came from."

"I'm sorry."

"Don't tell anybody what I told you, okay?"

"Okay."

There was silence for a time, neither of them knowing what else to say. All around them in the darkness were night sounds like nothing in our world. Squalls. Howls. Bone-chilling bird screeches. A fine rain began to fall.

"My dad embarrasses me sometimes, too," Emery said, finally. "He's not perfect. Nobody is. But I love him. He does the best he can. Besides, I'm not him. You're not your father, either. Things will get better for you."

"Sure, if I don't flunk out of school."

"I'll help you study," said Emery. "I promise."

"You'd do that?"

"Yeah."

Chippy studied Emery again, picking his nose. "Let me ask you somethin'."

"Sure."

"Why you study so hard? You always got your head in a book. You do it to show off? To suck up to the teachers? Is it 'cause you want to make a lot of money or somethin'?"

"No," said Emery. "Not for any of that. Knowledge is all I have. You take things away from me all the time. But nobody can ever take away what I know. Or what I can do. I love science because it's about evidence and truth. It doesn't care what color you are, or what country or culture you come from. Science is a way of life. A way of thinking about the world."

Chippy snorted, "Hmph. So you're sayin' mind beats muscle?"

"No, *you* said that. By the way, did you know each pound of muscle burns between thirty and fifty calories a day just by existing?"

"Thanks. I guess I needed to know that."

"Guys!" I shouted at the screen. "That's enough male bonding, don't you think?"

They laughed when they heard me. Then the growling of Chippy's stomach filled my ears. "You think there's any place around here to get somethin' to eat? Y'know, a burger joint?"

Emery and I exchanged glances, and I let him speak first. "Uh, we're in the Triassic period...."

"I know, you told me that already! Triassic, Dyassic, what difference does it

make? I'm starvin'! I haven't eaten all day. I'm so hongry, I could eat the butt off a dead bird."

That was the moment I realized Chippy really had slept through Mr. Tiplightly's class. "You can't get take-out in Pangaea," I said. "If you're hungry, you'll have to hunt and kill something yourself."

"Okay, no problem. I'm down for that. That's what I'll do then." Chippy looked for a sharp stick on the wet, spongy ground, found one, and tramped off through thistles, brambles, and slanting rain.

Outside, in the present, the disturbance grew louder.

I ran back to the window. The street overflowed with enough people to fill the

bleachers of our school's basketball court.
Police officers were struggling to keep them
back. My head began to feel tight. One of the
policemen, staring right at me, started
shouting into a megaphone: "You in the
house! Can you can hear me? I want you to
turn off the electric fence. Step outside with
both your hands in the air."

I tore myself away from the window,
feeling pressure in the lower part of me. I
needed to go to the bathroom really bad.
There was one down the hallway from
Emery's bedroom, so that's where I went,
closing the door so I couldn't hear the voices
calling me from outside. I sat alone in the
darkness. I sat there for a long, long time
and cried. I didn't want to leave the

bathroom. Or be arrested. Or expelled from school. I didn't want my life to be over at ten years old. I was wiping my eyes with toilet paper when a knock came at the door.

"Miss Gwen?" It was Cal. "You've been in there for half an hour. Is everything all right? Emery has been trying to reach you for the last five minutes. I think they've discovered something...unusual."

I forced myself to go back into Emery's bedroom and to that...Chronovisor. I could hear his voice even before I saw the screen, which had changed. It crackled with static. Snow like from a broken antenna. I could barely see the boys, but it looked like Chippy was cooking something impaled on a stick over a fire—a finless fish, maybe six inches

long, with thick plates on its head. It looked
like a big tadpole.

I asked, "You caught something
already?"

"If I'm hongry, I don't mess around,"
Chippy said. Their faces, streaked by sweat,
were lit by the lightbulb on Emery's belt.
Chippy nibbled at a piece of the fish. "Tastes
like tuna."

"That's an early cousin of an Astraspis,"
said Emery.

Chippy held up his catch. "You want
some?"

"I hate tuna. Might as well be Spam."
He swung his eyes back to the screen.
"Gabby, I know you can't see what I'm
looking at now..."

"I can see a little something, reflected in your glasses."

"Good. Because I can't describe it. The design of this thing is different from anything I've ever seen. Some of its elements don't appear on our periodic table. They must have been synthetically manufactured, but not here on Earth because hominids, our prehuman ancestors, won't appear for another 183 million years."

"Em, do you hear yourself? Please don't make me say the A-word. People think I'm weird enough already."

"Then don't use it. I just can't see any other explanation. Whoever put this here comes from an alien civilization thousands of years ahead of us.... Are you still there? You didn't pass out, did you? If you did, I'd understand."

"No, but I can barely hear you. And I'm trippin'. Where are these—I won't say it!— inventors now?"

"Not here, that's for sure. Maybe they had a colony, then left before they had time to build a second transceiver. Maybe they decided dinosaurs were as far as life on Earth would evolve. Or maybe carnivores ate them. Who knows? We can figure that out later. Right now we have a more serious problem."

"Talk louder. You're breaking up...."

"If what I'm seeing is right, this transceiver is powering down. It's shutting off. My guess is that it works in cycles, turning off for a period to rest. Or repair itself. We've been giving it a pretty good workout since this morning, and it's never been used before. I think we've got ten minutes before it turns off completely."

"There's something else—*there*—behind you."

They turned around, seeing what I saw. A herd of about twenty dragonlike dinosaurs was coming cautiously their way.

Chippy's knees knocked together. He dropped his fish. "Gizmo, I hope you brought more salad. They're vegetarians, right?"

"No. Those are Herrerasauruses. They're carnivores." Emery's nose pressed against the screen. "Gabby, this would be a very good time to activate the reverse sequence like I showed you."

"All right." I looked at the instrument panel. My mind was racing like the hamster Mr. Tiplightly kept in a cage in our classroom. I reached down for the notepad with Emery's instructions, and...

Half of it was gone. I'd placed it too close to the transceiver. (I never can remember that stuff about meters or how to convert them to feet.) The other half went back with Emery to the Triassic era.

No! I thought: *no!*

Cal rolled up behind me. "Miss Gwen...."

"Not now! I have to think!"

I squeezed shut my eyes. Twisting my fingers, I tried to remember what I'd written. Nothing came.

Nothing.

If you've ever folded your hands around a balloon, squeezing its thin skin, sinking your fingernails into it deeper and wondering how close it was to bursting, that's how I felt inside. I had failed them. They were trapped forever in the Triassic period. It was my fault.

My fault!

"Uh, Miss Gwen..."

"Shut up!" I said, and that was when I got so frustrated and angry at myself that I needed to kick something. So I kicked Cal, knocking him onto his side.

Quietly, he said, "I have the instructions."

"What?"

"I recorded them for you."

"Why didn't you say that before?"

"I believe you ordered me to—how did you put it?—button my lip, but insofar as I am a nonorganic mechanism not created to resemble a human being, that particular action isn't something that—"

"Just give me the sequence!" I tilted him upright. "Now! We only have two minutes left."

With Cal guiding me through every step, I poked keys, pushed levers, turned dials, and flipped switches. The room started to rumble, light ribboned from the transceiver. Time was twisting, turning on itself again. A blast of heat, like when you open a hot oven, burned my face. I whiffed the stench of swamp water and toadstools, the stinging smoke from the volcano. I started coughing, my eyes watering. Slowly, two shapes began to materialize in the glare. Then, at last, Emery and Chippy stood in front of us, dirty and dripping wet.

Chippy screamed when he realized where he was. He threw his arms around Emery in a bear hug that lifted him off the floor, squeezing him until Emery was cross-eyed. They both said at the same time:

"Good job, Gabby!"

"Gizmo, I'm never gonna call you Brickhead again!"

Chippy put Emery down. The front of him reeked from a big smudge of dinosaur poop. His trousers were torn. He looked tired. Then we heard a voice from behind us.

"It appears I'm late as usual and have missed all the fun."

There in the doorway, resting his weight on an owl-head walking stick, was Professor Haley.

"How did you get inside?" I asked.

"Oh, that was easy. When I got an off-the-grid message from Cal, I came right over, not to the front of the house but to the back. I helped Emery design this security system. I knew how to shut it off for a few seconds, step through when the police were preoccupied with people on the street, and turn it back on. You've got quite a crowd clamoring for you out there. Cal said something about time travel. Let me see what my reckless young friend has cooked up this time."

He pulled a pair of glasses from his coat pocket, slipped them on, then took a few moments to study the dual cylinders, the mirrors inside the transceiver, the blueprints, clucking his tongue with admiration. "This really *is* quite good. Emery, I've always known you were a genius, but you're brighter than I was at your age. And I was no dunderhead. You know I started classes at M.I.T. when I was ten, don't you, graduated when I was fourteen, and earned my Ph.D. in particle physics at eighteen. But I couldn't have come up with anything like this at that age. This is better than the nuclear fusion reactor you built two years ago. Just take a look at these nano-level transistors."

"Thank you, sir."

The Professor squinted, swinging his gaze toward Emery. "Don't congratulate yourself too quickly, young man. I wish you had informed me of what you were planning to do." Now his voice was stern. "Your trip to the Triassic period has probably triggered a splitting off of the you that went back in time from the you that didn't. I may not be exactly the Dangerfield Edison Haley I was before your little misadventure. But there's no way for me to know because most likely we're living in a new universe that you created. Only you three have the basis for recognizing those subtle changes. And I think you should keep it that way. It's best if your travels in time remain a secret. Can you invent a story to cover this up?"

"We did," I said. "Emery told Principal Jackson that Chippy might be playing hooky all day."

"I imagine that will suffice."

Chippy said, sheepishly, "Sometimes I *do* play hooky."

"I won't fool around with time again." Emery looked sideways, his eyes lowered. "I promise."

"Oh, you will in one of the other infinite, parallel universes. Just try not to do it again in this one." The Professor rumpled Emery's hair. "Perhaps you should go outside now. You need to let everyone know you're all right." His nose twitched. "After that, I suggest you and Chippy each take a shower."

This was the moment I'd been dreading all day. I walked downstairs behind Emery, still wearing only one shoe, thinking of all the chaos we'd created in less than twelve hours. I figured they were going to put us under the jail. I straightened his tie for him. Even though we were afraid, that made him smile. Emery opened the front door. He scooped my right hand into his left. We stepped side by side onto the front porch, our fingers intertwined, our heads held high. The October evening was warm. It was twilight, the sky blue and bottomless. An odor of dry leaves scented the air. Before us was a sea of faces like we were on stage, grabbing us with their eyes, reeling us in. All those people stared and were silent.

They were silent for seconds that felt like forever. Waiting for something. It was like the whole world was holding its breath.

I squeezed Emery's hand tighter. Then Chippy appeared behind us, safe and smiling. Waving and walking with the Professor's cane.

That's when they cheered.

Our families burst through the police line toward the porch. Everyone followed. A tsunami of people. I wondered: Did they miss Chippy that much? *Him?*

We were surrounded, engulfed by hugs and handshakes. Some people cried. Emery's mom encircled us with her arms, and a good-looking man I'd never seen before pulled Chippy toward him. He was large, with the look of someone who might have once been a heavyweight boxer. His short hair formed a silver halo around his head, and his dark suit was so perfectly molded to his body, it looked poured or painted on.

"I was afraid I'd lost you, son."

Chippy stepped back, squinting. "Do I know you?"

The man smiled, painfully. "I'm not surprised you'd say that. We don't know each other well enough—not since your mother and I separated. I was at the office when I heard about what happened at school. I was preparing for the Civil Rights case I have to argue before the Supreme Court tomorrow. My partner at the firm said she'd take my place. It's my fault we haven't spent enough time together. No father should miss a football game when his son is captain of the team."

"You're my father?" Chippy wobbled on his feet. "I'm captain of the freakin' football team?"

"You're much admired in our community. And if you give me a chance, I'm going to try to be a good father. You deserve that. Let's go home. We have a lot to talk about."

Emery and I were speechless. We watched them blend back into the crowd. Then we heard Cal clank onto the front porch.

> *By the look in his eyes, I'd say Chippy's*
> *   surprised.*
> *So here's what I suggest you do:*
> *Try to discover all the things that are new.*
> *Emery's dad has considerable ambition*
> *And works each day as a lab technician.*
> *His mother's got her life in order*
> *Pulling down good bread as a court reporter.*
> *Pookie and Toughie turned their lives around*
> *Like they were lost but now they're found.*

Pookie wins chess tournaments all over the state.
And Toughie does art that critics say is first-rate.

"Em," I said, "about Cal's lame raps..."

"I know. I'm going to program him with a rhyming dictionary. I've got some time to work on that now."

As things turned out, he did have time—two weeks, in fact, which is how long Principal Jackson suspended Emery and me for bringing to school an invention that blew itself to smithereens. But we didn't get expelled. Or go to jail. And a month later, we were back in Mr. Tiplightly's science class. Five minutes before the bell rang, he held up a drawing of a dinosaur.

"Can anyone identify this reptile and tell us its dietary preferences?"

No one spoke. Except for the whirring of the hamster in its cage, there wasn't a sound. Emery and I didn't say a word. We knew better. But Chippy's hand shot straight into the air.

"That's a Plateosaurus. Herbivores don't eat nothin' that has a face. Just veggies. And them Astraspis? They taste like tuna."

Mr. Tiplightly took a step back, surprised. "Well, I don't know what prehistoric fish tasted like, Mr. Payne, but that's right about Plateosauruses. Maybe there's hope for you yet. Did you learn that in our textbook?"

"Naw." He smiled at Emery and me. "But I know. Trust me."

Everywhere we looked, for days and weeks, we noticed differences caused by our trip through time. What we went through probably changed little details in your life, too. Think about it. Don't some things you remember from long ago seem like a dream, or maybe like they happened to someone else and you just heard about or imagined them? Or like you lived them in a different life? Every so often, some nights as I lie in bed before falling asleep, I can't help wondering about all those other possible universes where things probably turned out differently.

But that's a story for another time.

ABOUT THE AUTHORS

Elisheba Johnson, former owner and curator of Faire Gallery Cafe, is an Executive and Commissions Liaison for the Office of Arts and Culture in Seattle. She writes for *Curating a Life*, her parenting blog, and creates mixed media art pieces.

Dr. Charles Johnson is a novelist, essayist, literary critic, short-story writer, philosopher, and professor emeritus at the University of Washington, Seattle. He has published thousands of drawings as a cartoonist and illustrator, two collections, *Black Humor* (1970) and *Half-Past Nation Time* (1972), and created, co-produced, and hosted the 1970 PBS drawing program *Charlie's Pad*. Charles Johnson is a MacArthur fellow, the recipient of an American Academy of Arts and Letters Award for Literature, and a winner of the National Book Award for his novel *Middle Passage*.

ALSO BY CHARLES JOHNSON

FICTION

Dr. King's Refrigerator and Other Bedtime Stories

Soulcatcher and Other Stories

Dreamer

Middle Passage

The Sorcerer's Apprentice

Oxherding Tale

Faith and the Good Thing

PHILOSOPHY

Being and Race: Black Writing Since 1970

Philosophy: An Innovative Introduction: Fictive Narrative, Primary Texts, and Responsive Writing (with Michael Boylan)

NONFICTION

King: The Photobiography of Martin Luther King Jr.
(with Bob Adelman)

I Call Myself an Artist: Writings by and about Charles Johnson (edited by Rudolph Byrd)

Africans in America (with Patricia Smith)

Black Men Speaking (with John McCluskey Jr.)

Turning the Wheel: Essays on Buddhism and Writing

Passing the Three Gates: Interviews with Charles Johnson (edited by James McWilliams)

The Joy of Being Buddhist: Dharma Essays and Stories (forthcoming)

The Words and Wisdom of Charles Johnson (forthcoming)

DRAWINGS

Half-Past Nation Time

Black Humor

CPSIA information can be obtained at www.ICGtesting.com
Printed in the USA
BVOW07s0554241013

334509BV00001B/5/P

9 781620 151815